I060062b

The Exit Interview

by William Missouri Downs

A Samuel French Acting Edition

SAMUEL FRENCH

FOUNDED 1830

SAMUELFRENCH.COM

ISBN 978-0-573-70090-3   Printed in U.S.A.   #20383

MUSIC AND IMAGE USE NOTE

Licensees are solely responsible for obtaining formal written permission from copyright owners to use copyrighted music and images in the performance of this play and are strongly cautioned to do so. If no such permission is obtained by the licensee, then the licensee must use only original music and images that the licensee owns and controls. Licensees are solely responsible and liable for all music and image clearances and shall indemnify the copyright owners of the play and their licensing agent, Samuel French, Inc., against any costs, expenses, losses and liabilities arising from the use of music and images by licensees.

IMPORTANT BILLING AND CREDIT REQUIREMENTS

All producers of *THE EXIT INTERVIEW* must give credit to the Author of the Play in all programs distributed in connection with performances of the Play, and in all instances in which the title of the Play appears for the purposes of advertising, publicizing or otherwise exploiting the Play and/or a production. The name of the Author *must* appear on a separate line on which no other name appears, immediately following the title and *must* appear in size of type not less than fifty percent of the size of the title type.

THE EXIT INTERVIEW was first produced as part of a Rolling World Premiere by Orlando Shakespeare Theater, Sand Diego REPertory Theatre, InterAct Theatre Company, Riverside Theatre, Actor's Theatre of Charlotte, and Salt Lake Acting Company as part of the National New Play Network's Continued Life program.

THE EXIT INTERVIEW was developed at the Orlando Shakespeare Theater's Harriett Lake Festival of New Plays. The Orlando Shakespeare Theater, in partnership with UCF, also staged its world premiere on September 29, 2012. It was directed by Patrick Flick. The set was designed by Robin Watts, the costumes were designed by Corinne Walsh, the lighting was designed by Mary Heffernan, and the sound was designed by Britt Sandusky. The stage manager was Melissa E. Koerner. The cast was as follows:

DICK FIG	Michael Marinaccio
EUNICE	Anitra Pritchard
ACTRESS #1	Lauren Butler
ACTRESS #2	Janine Klein
ACTOR #1	Nathan Sebens
ACTOR #2	Alexander Mrazek

CHARACTERS

DICK FIG - A young college professor with his leg in a cast - His PhD was on Bertolt Brecht

EUNICE - A pawn in the human resources department

ACTRESS #1

    CHEERLEADER #1 - With pompoms

    MARY - An oboe player - Dick's ex-girlfriend

    SAMANTHA - A mother with a baby carriage

    BUSINESSWOMAN #2 - An expert on underwear

    DR. DOBSON - PhD in religious studies from Yale

ACTRESS #2

    CHEERLEADER #2 - With pompoms

    MRS. MEREDITH - Mary's mother

    CHLOE - Eunice's young assistant

    A MAKEUP LADY - She can make you look good

    BETH - A mother with a baby carriage

    BUSINESSWOMAN IN A BRA - An expert on bras

    LADY NEWSCASTER - Foxy Fox Newscaster

    ACTRESS #1 - Bertolt Brecht announcer

    DR. KATTS - A distinguished scientist

ACTOR #1

    MASKED GUNMAN - Who has killed ten people

    ACTOR #1 - Bertolt Brecht announcer

    A PRIEST - A celibate

    BUSINESSMAN #1 - An expert on underwear

    DR. HUBERT - President of the LDS Church

    HANK STARLING - A professional baseball player

ACTOR #2

    WALTER - Foxy Fox Newscaster

    BUSINESSMAN #2 - An expert on underwear

    DR. JAEGER - A distinguished scientist

    ACTOR #2 - Bertolt Brecht announcer

Please Note: this play can be produced with a much larger cast.

SETTING

A theatre - The theatrical lights and bare walls of the stage are exposed. Scenes can be staged with as little as a few chairs and a desk – or, money allowing, a series of platforms. Whatever you do, never let the audience forget they're in a theatre.

Above the stage is a projection screen where scene titles appear. This projection screen represents god, and this play tilts away from realism.

The walls of the theatre, even those around the audience, are covered with banners and slogans:

Nature vs. Scripture
Create your purpose vs. Follow God's purpose
Human needs vs. God's needs
Humans are capable vs. Humans are imperfect
I did it! vs. God did it!
I did it! vs. The devil made me do it!
Many books vs. One book
Research vs. Revelation
The world happened vs. The world is designed
Observation vs. Theology
All people vs. Chosen people
Now vs. Later

Mixed in are:
Pepsi vs. Coke
Boxers vs. Briefs
Mac vs. PC
Honda vs. Toyota
Big Mac vs. Whopper

AUTHOR'S NOTES

This play contains several advertisements in the second act. Some of these ads are projected from the screen above the stage; others are contained within the dialogue. If the theatre finds local businesses or organizations that would like to buy one of these advertisements, that section of the script may be rewritten to accommodate.

For more information about the play, including script updates, photos, production designs, interviews and notes, visit *The Exit Interview* website: www.uwyo.edu/thd2/downs/exit.htm.

ACKNOWLEDGEMENTS

Special thanks to: Patrick Flick, Jim Helsinger, Jason Loewith, Seth Rozin, Sam Woodhouse, Jody Hovland, Dan Shoemaker, Lou Anne Wright, Jojo Ruf, Michael Mainaccio, and Kelie Rae Rockey.

ACT ONE

(Raucous Rock and Roll. The screen above the stage doesn't just light up, it's a technical event as it oscillates to life. It reads:)

Warning Labels!

*(Two effervescent college **CHEERLEADERS** complete with pompoms enter cheering. They're followed by a ski-masked **GUNMAN** – He doesn't react; he stands unassumingly in the background pointing his gun in their direction, and listening to an iPod.)*

CHEERLEADER #1. *(bubbly)* Welcome, Ladies and Gentlemen!

CHEERLEADER #2. *(spirited)* Are you ready!

CHEERLEADER #1. Give me an "O!" Come on give me an "O!"

(They prompt the audience to respond.)

AUDIENCE. O!

CHEERLEADER #2. Give me an "F!"

AUDIENCE. F!

CHEERLEADER #1. Give me another "F!"

AUDIENCE. F!

CHEERLEADER #2. Give me an "E!"

AUDIENCE. E!

CHEERLEADER #1. Give me an "N!"

AUDIENCE. N!

CHEERLEADER #2. Give me an "S!"

AUDIENCE. S!

CHEERLEADER #1. Give me an "I!"

AUDIENCE. I!

CHEERLEADER #2. Give me a "V!"

AUDIENCE. V!

CHEERLEADER #1. Give me an "E!"

AUDIENCE. E!

CHEERLEADER #1. What's that spell?

CHEERLEADER #2. Offensive! Offensive! This play is Offensive!

(They chest bump.)

BOTH. Yeaaaaaaaaa!

CHEERLEADER #1. Before we start. Please take a moment to off your cells and pagers!

CHEERLEADER #2. Cell phones totally off!

CHEERLEADER #1. Also, for those of you under the age of thirty–.

CHEERLEADER #2. Yeaaaaa under thirty!

CHEERLEADER #1. Please know that it's considered rude to text or twitter during a play.

CHEERLEADER #2. That's right! It's time to grow up and admit that no one gives a flying crap about what you're doing right now!

CHEERLEADER #1. The opinions expressed in this play do not necessarily reflect the views of _____ *(fill in the name of your theatre)*!

CHEERLEADER #2. Let's hear it for _____ *(fill in the name of your theatre)*!

BOTH. Yeaaaaa!

CHEERLEADER #1. This play is not suitable for viewers who find any of the following objectionable:

CHEERLEADER #2. Gun violence! Bang! Bang!

CHEERLEADER #1. Women in the workplace! Yea!

CHEERLEADER #2. Soccer moms discussing scientific method!

CHEERLEADER #1. Criticism of Fox News!

CHEERLEADER #2. Candid discussions on religion and politics!

CHEERLEADER #1. Priests defending the Holy Trinity using perplexing analogies!

CHEERLEADER #2. Plane crashes!

CHEERLEADER #1. *(upbeat)* With no survivors!

CHEERLEADER #2. School shootings!

CHEERLEADER #1. *(joyous)* With few survivors!

CHEERLEADER #2. Babies being run over by trains!

CHEERLEADER #1. Or Lutheranism!

CHEERLEADER #2. Or audience members who think realism is the only kinda theatre.

CHEERLEADER #1. Boo! Realism!

CHEERLEADER #2. This play contains Brechtian Alienation devices! Yeaaaaa! Bertolt Brecht–!

CHEERLEADER #1. Who's Bertolt Brecht?

CHEERLEADER #2. I have no idea! But I'll bet he'll make this play offensive!

BOTH. Yeaaaaaaaaa!

(They chest bump.)

CHEERLEADER #1. The management is not responsible for:

CHEERLEADER #2. Lost items!

CHEERLEADER #1. Misplaced tickets!

CHEERLEADER #2. Or any existential uncertainty or metaphysical isolation that may result!

CHEERLEADER #1. Let's hear it for existential uncertainty!

BOTH. *(prompting the audience to cheer)* Yeaaaaaaaaa!

CHEERLEADER #1. And metaphysical isolation!

BOTH. *(shaking their pompoms)* Yeaaaaaaaaa!

CHEERLEADER #2. This play contains over twenty characters!

CHEERLEADER #1. Which is a real problem because this theatre can't afford to pay twenty actors!*

CHEERLEADER #2. Yeaaaaaaaaa actors!

CHEERLEADER #1. So all the roles will be played by only six actors!

---

* Please note: These lines may be altered to match the size of your cast.

BOTH. So deal with it!

CHEERLEADER #1. Are we done?

CHEERLEADER #2. Totally!

CHEERLEADER #1. Ready? Hit it! *(prompting the audience to cheer)* Give me an "E!"

AUDIENCE. E!

CHEERLEADER #2. Explicit content!

CHEERLEADER #1. Give me a "V!"

AUDIENCE. V!

CHEERLEADER #2. A whole bunch of violence!

CHEERLEADER #1. Give me an "L!"

AUDIENCE. L!

CHEERLEADER #2. Lutheranism!

CHEERLEADER #1. Give me an "A!"

AUDIENCE. A!

CHEERLEADER #2. Adult themes!

CHEERLEADER #1. Put it all together and what's it spell?

BOTH. *(after the audience's failed attempt)* Yeeeeeeeea!

CHEERLEADER #1. Enjoy!

BOTH. *(shaking their pompoms)* Yeeeeeeeea!

*(Pompom shaking exit. The **GUNMAN** quietly follows them off.)*

(Transitions to new scenes are filled with rock and roll music and lights. The sign jumps to life. It reads:)

Last Day On The Job!

*(Lights up on **EUNICE**, a dry, professional human resources administrator sitting at her desk. Her latest case is **DICK**, a young professorish-type. **DICK** sports a large cast on his leg/foot and crutches.)*

EUNICE. And how are we today?

DICK. Fine.

EUNICE. Can you believe all this rain?

DICK. *(uncomfortable with small talk)* Sure is rainy.

EUNICE. I heard we might have more.

DICK. I suppose.

EUNICE. *(off his cast)* Skiing accident?

DICK. No.

EUNICE. Auto?

DICK. It's complicated.

EUNICE. I broke my big toe once. *(beat)* Skiing. Painful. Very painful.

DICK. If I may be honest–.

EUNICE. We're all about honesty here.

DICK. I'm kinda not into small talk.

EUNICE. Small what?

DICK. You know – How's the weather? What did I do to my foot? I don't mean to be rude. I'm being pink-slipped because of budget cuts and talking about the weather isn't going to make me feel better.

EUNICE. When one is transitioning-and-broadening-their-field-of-endeavor there can be pain and deep resentment. Just remember when God closes a door he opens a skylight.

DICK. Question–.

EUNICE. Yes, free psychological counseling is available through our secure website. Shall we begin? You are Dick Fig. Correct?

DICK. Richard.

EUNICE. It's says you're a "Dick".

DICK. I go by Richard.

EUNICE. *(writing on the form)* Question number one: besides petty politics what did you find least satisfying about your job?

DICK. Besides petty politics?

EUNICE. You were a non-tenured instructor at a university; they just assume there was petty politics.

DICK. Besides petty politics, I'd have to say – the exit interview.

EUNICE. *(un-amused)* You're being funny.

DICK. Just a little joke.

EUNICE. I've noticed that funny people are, more often than not, hiding their pain. Comedy comes from pain doesn't it?

DICK. True. That's why so many standup comedians come from Somalia.

(Beat. The stone-faced **EUNICE** *writes a note on the form.)*

EUNICE. Note: sense of humor.

DICK. What're you...?

EUNICE. There's a little side box here on the form and I'm noting that you have a sense of humor.

DICK. Why?

EUNICE. This way the higher ups get a sense for the personage. It helps them understand what transpired. For example if I noted "ruffled" they'd take that into account when they evaluate the results.

DICK. And what does "ruffled" mean?

EUNICE. Ruffled means that the interviewee more than likely has exaggerated complaints and feelings of inferiority.

DICK. And "sense of humor"?

EUNICE. Just a note.

DICK. But it must mean something–.

EUNICE. You're taking this far too seriously.

DICK. Just wondering...

EUNICE. Fine – a notation of "sense of humor" means that the interviewee is less than serious and that his answers should be given little or no weight. Perhaps even discarded if the attempts at humor continue.

DICK. My answers won't be taken seriously?

EUNICE. Let's not get ruffled.

*(***CHLOE*** rushes in.)*

(We hear the offstage **CHEERLEADERS**.*)*

OFFSTAGE CHEERLEADERS. *(This cheer repeats as needed.)* Hey, Hey, Hey! Be aggressive *(clap clap clap)* It's not over! *(clap)* Till it's over! *(clap clap)* It's not over! *(clap)* Till it's over!

EUNICE. Door!

*(***CHLOE*** *closes the door. The* **CHEERLEADERS** *fade.)*

CHLOE. There's a student here–.

EUNICE. Appointment?

CHLOE. No, but he's really insistent.

EUNICE. You know the rules, no appointment means–.

CHLOE. He doesn't want to see *you*; says he has a meeting with Dick.

DICK. Richard.

CHLOE. You were supposed to've read his short story or something?

DICK. Oh. Forgot. Would you tell...ah...

CHLOE. Noah.

DICK. Would you tell Noah that I'm no longer employed by the university.

CHLOE. But this guy is really making me uncomfortable.

EUNICE. What did I say this morning? Be...

CHLOE. Aaaammmmmmm...decisive?

EUNICE. There're plenty of other students who'd kill to have this work/study job.

(Frustrated, **CHLOE** *opens the door.)*

OFFSTAGE CHEERLEADERS. *(This cheer repeats as needed.)* We're number one! Can't be number two! And we're going to beat the whoopsie out of you!

EUNICE. Door!

*(***CHLOE*** *exits. The* **CHEERLEADERS** *fade.)*

---

*The Cheerleaders will have to be recorded to keep within only six actors.

EUNICE. Question number two: do you have any broad-spectrum complaints?

DICK. Broad-spectrum?

EUNICE. *(rapid fire)* For example, the university, for no apparent reason, moved me to this office. A former storage room that smells of chlorine. But there's little I can do 'cause there's no window. It's been two weeks and it still says "storage room" on the door and the lock is broken. To top it off, they put me across the hall from the Cheerleader Captain's office. If I hear him yell one more time, "Be authentic!" I might just never stop throwing up. If this were my exit interview, that'd be my broad-spectrum complaint.

DICK. I have no–.

(**EUNICE** *checks a box on the form.*)

EUNICE. Three: now that you are transitioning-and-broadening-your-field-of-endeavor, who is your new employer?

DICK. None, I guess I'll be self-employed.

EUNICE. *(filling out the form)* Unemployed.

DICK. No, self–. I've written a book. Coming out next month. Confidentially–.

EUNICE. Everything here is confidential.

DICK. I just happened to have a friend of a friend who works at *The New York Times.* He thinks they're going to review it. My agent's assistant – who's probably wildly overestimating – says that it's entirely possible that I'll be in *The Times* top ten list within a matter of months.

EUNICE. Congratulations. I make it a habit to read every book on *The Times* top ten list.

DICK. Really. Every book.

EUNICE. Well, most…several…three–. What's yours about?

DICK. It's about the chaos of the human soul and the emptiness of the Copernican universe.

EUNICE. *(counterfeit)* That has bestseller written all over it.

DICK. Technically it's not about chaos or emptiness. It's more about Bertolt Brecht and how there's no divine presence in the universe, and that humans have little or no significant meaning in the vast cosmos.

EUNICE. Bertolt who?

DICK. *(He can't help but sound PhD-ish.)* Brecht – an influential playwright, director. Brecht felt the objective discernment that autonomous artworks presuppose in the viewer was inadequate while his didactic style reinforced his communist perspective. It's loosely based on my PhD thesis. It's called *No Religion, No Politics.*

EUNICE. I don't get it.

DICK. Those are the two things you're not allowed to talk about in polite society anymore. The title came from my girlfriend–. I should say, ex-girlfriend. When we used to go to her mother's – just before she'd open the door – Mary would squeeze my hand and say, "No religion, no politics." Two subjects we *should* be talking about but don't because it's considered impolite – even politically incorrect. So instead we engage in trivial small talk about things like the weather. Today she'd say, "No religion, no politics, no global warming–."

(During this next section **EUNICE** *professionally checks off the answers on the form.)*

EUNICE. *(cold)* There's that sense of humor again. *(She notes it.)* Next section. Rapid fire. "Yes." "No." Don't think, don't try to be funny, just answer. Ready. Go. Do you have any parking tickets?

DICK. No. Wait. No. Yes…no.

EUNICE. Do you have any overdue library books?

DICK. No.

EUNICE. Would you recommend this university to a friend?

DICK. No–. I mean, yes.

EUNICE. If you were a snowflake would you look forward to melting?

DICK. …ah–?

EUNICE. You're thinking.

DICK. What kind of–?

EUNICE. No think-think.

DICK. Maybe?

EUNICE. That's not a box on the form.

DICK. Okay, yes, no, yes–.

EUNICE. Were you pleased with the parking situation on campus?

DICK. That's a loaded question.

EUNICE. Excuse me?

DICK. That's known as a loaded question. All the others were simple "Yes" or "No" but this one has the word "pleased" located within it. "Were you *pleased* with the parking situation…"

(Beat – EUNICE studies him.)

EUNICE. We're feeling hostility aren't we.

DICK. No. It's just that the administration obviously wants a positive response. It's known as a loaded question…an unloaded would be, "What do you think of the parking situation?" See, that's unloaded.

(Beat. EUNICE blankly stares at him. He gives up.)

DICK. Yes, I was pleased with the parking.

EUNICE. If your bride said, "But my first love is the oboe," would you still marry?

DICK. Wait–.

EUNICE. I don't write the questions.

DICK. Obviously they've come up with some sort of peculiar psychological–. What do they hope to prove by asking if I'd marry an oboe player–?

EUNICE. You're reading into the question. It doesn't say she *is* an oboe player. It says she has deep affections for the oboe. More than she has for you.

DICK. No, if a woman loved her oboe more than me I wouldn't–.

EUNICE. We're positive?

DICK. Yes.

EUNICE. I'm not supposed to say this but…no one who has ever answered "no" to that question has ever been re–hired–. Why don't we come back to it.

DICK. No–. If a woman told me that she loved her oboe more than me I wouldn't get married. Final answer!

*(***CHLOE*** *enters with the student's short story. As she opens and closes the door the* ***CHEERLEADERS*** *fade in and out.)*

OFFSTAGE CHEERLEADERS. *(This cheer repeats as needed.)* Trip'm, Kick'm, Smack'm in the head! Don't let up till you know they're–good–n–dead!

CHLOE. Problem–!

EUNICE. Door.

CHLOE. This student is rather insistent–!

EUNICE. Door!

*(***CHLOE*** *closes the door.)*

CHLOE. Couldn't Dick just–.

DICK. Sure.

EUNICE. No. Classes are over.

CHLOE. But–.

DICK. It's really okay.

EUNICE. A writer needs to read great writing – to be inspired. But student writing – year in and year out – must be like death by a thousand cuts! Am I right?

DICK. In the ballpark.

CHLOE. You want me to tell him that?

EUNICE. Word for word.

(Frustrated, ***CHLOE*** *exits.)*

OFFSTAGE CHEERLEADERS. Strawberry shortcake, banana split – We think your team plays like shi-shake it to the left, shake it to the right, sit down, stand up, Fight, fight, fight!!

(The door closes and the **CHEERLEADERS** *fade.)*

DICK. Question–.

EUNICE. You're not allowed to ask questions until page six–.

DICK. Just one–.

EUNICE. But you're not–.

DICK. Hold on! *(beat)* How did you know my ex-girlfriend played the oboe?

(Rock and roll music and lights. The screen throbs to life. It reads:)

A Train Ran Over My Baby!

(A makeup room.)

(Beside **MARY** *are a baby carriage and an oboe case. Her arm is in a sling.* **WALTER**, *a hurried handsome newscaster, enters. During this scene he is constantly texting.)*

WALTER. *(hurried)* Wow, you look unremarkable, I mean after...

MARY. Thank you–.

WALTER. And the train never touched your...

MARY. A small scratch on his–.

WALTER. But your arm.

MARY. Oh. Unrelated.

WALTER. Ever done T.V. before?

MARY. First–.

WALTER. Few tips: stay calm, connect with me not the camera, don't slouch, and keep your responses to eight seconds or less.

(The **MAKEUP LADY** *enters. During the following she professionally touches up* **WALTER**'s *makeup and hair. She is constantly texting.)*

WALTER. Cut to the chase – tell me a story.

MARY. Well…I was sorta preoccupied–.

WALTER. Aren't we all.

MARY. Was rushing up to the metro station platform–.

WALTER. And before you knew it…

MARY. Was trying to hold his bottle in my right hand and my oboe in my left–.

WALTER. When suddenly…

MARY. The baby carriage just started rolling and–.

WALTER. Then all hell broke lose.

MARY. Didn't know that the wheel-lock was–.

WALTER. Wow, great story, but let's not talk about it on air. We've been looping the metro station security video from the incident for two days. I think our viewers'll find it more entertaining if you talk about *why* this happened.

MARY. The lock was broken and my oboe–.

WALTER. No, I mean the bigger picture.

MARY. I had too many things in my hands and then the baby carriage started rolling and–.

WALTER. You suddenly you knew that God had a purpose for your son. Right?

MARY. I–.

WALTER. Few years ago, remember that Airbus that went down in Queens, or Brooklyn?

MARY. I guess–.

WALTER. Got an exclusive one-on-one with a man who missed the plane–. Ran up just as they were closing the door. Missed an all important job interview that would've changed his life. Was filling out a complaint form at the service desk when the news came that the flight, *his* flight, had gone in. Smoldering wreckage, *total carnage* – but great video – he said that he knew in his heart that he had been spared because God had a purpose for him.

MARY. So, you want me to–.

WALTER. You don't have to know what that purpose is, that'd be presumptive on your part.

MARY. But what if I don't–.

WALTER. You don't thank God for saving your son?

MARY. Sure–.

WALTER. Let me tell you something about this medium. War is better than peace, violent protests better than nonviolent sit-ins, louder better than soft, emotion better than reason, L. Ron Hubbard better than Buddhists.

MARY. So you want me to–.

WALTER. Tell'em what you really think.

MARY. Which is–?

WALTER. God has a purpose for your son. Why else did he allow him to live?

MARY. I just thought it would be kinda cool to be on T.V.–.

WALTER. You thought it would be cool… *(chuckling with the* **MAKEUP LADY***)* She thought it would be cool. *(He pulls himself together.)* I'll introduce you and you'll say…

MARY. But what about all those baby carriages that fall in front of commuter trains and the baby *is* killed. What's God's purpose–?

WALTER. We'd never put that on air. That's what newspapers are for.

(The **MAKEUP LADY** *holds a mirror in front of* **WALTER***.)*

Good. Now let's help her a little. Maybe some rings around the eyes.

*(***WALTER** *pulls the tissue from his shirt collar.)*

Wanta know the truth? That guy, the one I interviewed, the one who missed the plane – my brother.

MARY. You're kidding.

WALTER. Three seconds late – slammed the door in his face.

MARY. Wow. And he…?

WALTER. Died six months later – pancreatic cancer.

MARY. So…God's purpose for your brother was–.

WALTER. Apparently so.

MARY. But–.

WALTER. Who am I to question the higher ups.

MARY. By "higher ups" you mean–? *(She indicates the heavens.)*

WALTER. Yep, the management of *Fox News*.

*(**WALTER** takes **MARY**'s hand.)*

(taking her into his confidence) Look, just between us, I know why my brother died.

MARY. You do?

WALTER. We were twins. Inseparable. By taking my brother, God let me know that he wanted me to be strong – to be my own man. Now you gotta understand why God let this little bundle of joy survive. What's its name?

MARY. Ben.

WALTER. He could've *(snaps his fingers)* with a blink…so why not?

MARY. I…

WALTER. You can do it.

MARY. *(guessing)* He…wanted me to go on TV and warn mothers about defective Chinese made baby carriages–?

WALTER. Nope. News Corp is trying to get a new cable link set up in Shanghai so we can't mention China for three weeks.

*(**WALTER** flips out his cell and hits auto dial.)*

(into cell phone) It's me. I think we should do the miracle baby story as a tape. We may want to edit this one… cause I'm detecting something…not much, but there is just a modicum of…that's right. Doubt…what? … Why didn't you tell me? *(hangs up)* Pleasure, gotta run. There's a gunman over at the campus. We're going to break in live. If you can stay around we'll try to tape you during a network break. *(to the **MAKEUP LADY**)* Better give me a once-over. Neck? I'm sure they'll want to go national.

(The **MAKEUP LADY** *checks him.)*

WALTER. Showtime.

*(***WALTER** *exits.* **MARY** *sits dumbfounded.)*

MAKEUP LADY. You okay?

MARY. *(concerned)* My ex-boyfriend teaches at the College. Today was his last day.

MAKEUP LADY. Wow. Think he's there now? You should text him.

MARY. He doesn't believe in cell phones.

MAKEUP LADY. No cell, wow. What is he, like, really really old?

(Rock and roll music and lights. The sign jerks to life. It reads:)

The Secret of the Secret

(And we are back in the exit interview.)

EUNICE. I'm sorry that your ex-girlfriend played the oboe – that must've been very painful for you.

DICK. When you're in love you put up with a lot–.

EUNICE. You know what you need? *The Secret.*

DICK. What secret?

EUNICE. You're a writer and you haven't read *The Secret* by Rhonda Byrne? – Was on *The New York Times* top ten list. And it was featured on Oprah – twice. It's great. You can master your destiny by just thinking–.

DICK. Please don't tell me that you believe–.

EUNICE. *The Secret?* It cured my cancer.

DICK. …Cancer?

EUNICE. Terminal lung cancer. Been cancer free for two years.

DICK. C'mon, they did something else…radiation–?

EUNICE. I prayed.

DICK. And your cancer…completely and totally–.

EUNICE. Had a spot on my lung and when I went in for further tests–.

DICK. Wait, you make it sound like you had full blown malignancy. You had–.

EUNICE. Cancer and I used *The Secret*'s laws of attraction to–.

DICK. You're doing it! Exactly what my book is about. You don't know if the spot was cancerous. It may have been a normal biological occurrence–.

EUNICE. I'm cured. Two years!

DICK. You're telling me with the help of a book you aligned the forces of the universe–.

EUNICE. It wasn't that easy. I had to make a collage.

DICK. A what?

EUNICE. You cut out of magazines the type of life you want, and then you paste it to poster board, although I found that foam board works better, and then you look at it each day and imagine yourself living that life.

DICK. ...I don't follow.

EUNICE. I have mine right here.

(EUNICE takes out a large collage on which she has pasted her hopes and dreams. During the following she points at the various dreams she has cut out of magazines.)

EUNICE. Here is the chlorine–free office I'll have some day. Here is my future Porsche. Here is where I'll travel once I become fluent in French and Italian. And this little blob down here represents the weight I'm going to lose, after which I will write a bestselling memoir, which is represented by this book right here. It's going to be about forgiveness.

DICK. *(not able to get his head around this)* You...you think you can make a collage, and think about it, and–.

EUNICE. I won an award for this collage. I was even interviewed on Fox News–.

(a far off gunshot)

DICK. What the hell...

EUNICE. *(doubting)* Thunder?

DICK. Don't think so.

EUNICE. Backfire?

DICK. Doubt it.

(another gunshot)

EUNICE. That's it. Car. Trust me. Happens all the time. The Cheerleader Captain has a crappy car. Back to work, next question. *(reading)* If you were going to be trapped on a desert island and you could take only one book. What book would you take?

DICK. Ah…

EUNICE. *(hopeful)* Yes?

DICK. …I'd take a book on how to survive on a desert island.

(Loud Rock and Roll, the lights shift. The sign springs to life. It reads:)

No Religion, No Politics

*(**MARY** walks into a special light – this time her arm is not in a sling, nor does she have the baby carriage.)*

MARY. You knew it was a gunshot. You weren't being honest with yourself, but you knew it.

DICK. Yes. I knew it.

MARY. And what were you doing, talking about a spot on her lung. People want to believe what they believe–.

DICK. At least I can–.

MARY. That's why we failed.

DICK. Because I–?

MARY. No, because you can't keep your mouth shut.

DICK. I admit it; it wasn't my finest hour–.

*(In this reality, **DICK** pops off his foot cast and joins **MARY**.)*

MARY. My poor mother. All she wanted–.

DICK. I was young–.

MARY. It was eighteen months ago!

(A doorbell. Lights up on **MRS. MEREDITH**, *Mary's mother – if anyone owns an Emily Post Etiquette book it's her. She enters wearing an apron and carrying a fancy tea set.)*

MARY. Look at her, she even polished grandma's silver.

DICK. Everything would've gone fine if you hadn't given me the manuscript.

MARY. Of course it's my fault.

(a doorbell)

MRS. MEREDITH. Coming!

*(***MARY*** and* **DICK** *hold hands, and join the scene. It is eighteen months earlier.)*

*(***MRS. MEREDITH*** runs out taking off her apron.)*

MARY. Relax. *(squeezing his hand)* She's a little set in her ways so be nice–. Oh, I forgot. They sent back the manuscript and your editor called. She wants a few changes.

(She takes his book manuscript from her purse. **DICK** *inspects it.)*

DICK. Changes. What changes?

MARY. Nothing major, she just wants you to cut out the part about small talk.

DICK. That's half the book.

MARY. Don't over react.

DICK. *(looking at the manuscript)* It's all red marks.

(Doorbell. **MRS. MEREDITH** *re-enters primping.)*

MARY. It's Thanksgiving – promise – no religion, no politics.

*(***MRS. MEREDITH*** walks up and hugs her daughter.)*

MRS. MEREDITH. My sweet little–. This must be Mr. Dick.

DICK. Richard Fig. Hello, Mrs. Meredith.

MRS. MEREDITH. Call me "Mom". *(to* **MARY***)* Am I right? *(to* **DICK***)* Come. Sit. Mary has said so many wonderful–. Can I get you something? Coffee?

MARY. Richard doesn't drink coffee, Mom.

MRS. MEREDITH. Probably best – stains your teeth and you have such nice—. How about a glass of milk?

MARY. He doesn't drink milk either. The pasteurization process overstresses the pancreas.

MRS. MEREDITH. I don't want you to have an overstressed pancreas.

MARY. He'd love a little carrot juice.

MRS. MEREDITH. Ah...I don't think we–.

MARY. Got carrots?

MRS. MEREDITH. I guess–.

MARY. Still got that old juicer?

MRS. MEREDITH. Haven't used it in–.

MARY. Then you got carrot juice. Right back. You two... You know...

(**MARY** *exits. Awkward pause.*)

MRS. MEREDITH. Can you believe all this rain?

DICK. Excuse me?

MRS. MEREDITH. We're having a lot of rain.

DICK. ...Yes.

MRS. MEREDITH. I heard we might have more. Rain is... (*beat*) ...good.

DICK. Yes.

MRS. MEREDITH. Oh! And Merry Christmas.

DICK. ...Thanks.

MRS. MEREDITH. What're you doing for Christmas?

DICK. ...Ah, nothing...

MRS. MEREDITH. Heard it might rain this Christmas season. What've you heard?

DICK. Mrs. Meredith–.

MRS. MEREDITH. Mom.

DICK. Mom...I think it's important to let you know that–.

MRS. MEREDITH. Mary told me. You detest idle chat. I disagree. I find it a useful talent. I mean to be able to speak and not really say anything is an art. Am I right?

DICK. ...No.

MRS. MEREDITH. *(not listening)* I even read a book on the subject. *Grace and Diplomacy – The Art of Small Talk.*

DICK. …Mrs. Meredith–.

MRS. MEREDITH. Mom.

DICK. About Christmas–.

MRS. MEREDITH. I agree, we're going to have a rainy Christmas.–.

DICK. No. …What I wanted to say is that I don't celebrate Christmas

MRS. MEREDITH. Pardon?

DICK. I'm not Christian.

MRS. MEREDITH. *(concerned)* …Mary failed to inform me… Happy Hanukah.

DICK. I'm not Jewish either.

MRS. MEREDITH. I don't suppose "Happy Kwanzaa" is called for?

DICK. I'm not anything.

MRS. MEREDITH. Oh. You have my condolences.

DICK. Truth is, I'm in the theatre.

MRS. MEREDITH. Yes, Mary mentioned you recently finished your PhD on Berky?

DICK. Brecht.

MRS. MEREDITH. *(She has no idea who he is.)* Brecht, right.

DICK. Brecht felt the objective discernment that autonomous artworks presuppose–. *(He stops and reconsiders.)* What I'm trying to say is that he eliminated the vicarious experience from the theatre by using various staging techniques to remind the audience that they were in a theatre.

MRS. MEREDITH. *(lost)* Okay.

DICK. He felt that theatre shouldn't be magical, i.e., it shouldn't just help us escape reality, but make us think. He did this sometimes by stopping a play in the middle and putting on a completely different play, or by having the characters break in to song for no reason.

MRS. MEREDITH. *(pouring tea)* That's so interesting…so, do you think we'll have more rain?

DICK. Look, Mrs. Meredith, Mom, I just want you to know that I don't celebrate Christmas because when Christians took power at the end of the Roman Empire they cancelled the theatre for nearly four hundred years.

MRS. MEREDITH. Did they now.

DICK. I must also tell you that we are not that into Thanksgiving.

MRS. MEREDITH. We?

DICK. Mary and I.

MRS. MEREDITH. Because…

DICK. We don't think pilgrims are anything to celebrate. Before they came to America they were called Puritans in England. It was the Puritans who tore Shakespeare's Globe to the ground.

MRS. MEREDITH. Is there anything you *do* celebrate?

DICK. The Winter Solstice.

MRS. MEREDITH. *(still trying to be nice)* And how do we celebrate – Human sacrifice?

DICK. We light candles, read poems to each other, and then Mary plays her oboe.

MRS. MEREDITH. I don't mean to be apathetic but you do know that my daughter was raised Presbyterian.

(A loud whine – it's the old juicer. They wait. It stops.)

And Presbyterians are "into" Thanksgiving, not to mention the birthday of our Lord and Savior.

(A louder whine, higher pitched this time – It's really straining. They wait. It scrapes to a stop.)

And not so much into carrot juice.

DICK. My intention is not to offend.

MRS. MEREDITH. Of course not.

DICK. I just thought it would be best to talk about this right away rather than years from now after we've had children.

MRS. MEREDITH. And how do you intend to raise the little heathens?

DICK. We're going to teach them about all faiths and alternatives.

MRS. MEREDITH. Alternatives?

DICK. Atheism, agnosticism, humanism, deism. Now isn't this better than talking about the weather? I mean we live in this age where religion is a conversation stopper. But I can tell that you're open to real talk.

MRS. MEREDITH. *(holding back)* You're telling me that at my daughter's wedding there will be no...God.

DICK. No. I'm saying there will be no wedding. Mary and I are protesting the institution of marriage. As long as gays and lesbians can't we won't–.

(A loud whine – it's the juicer. They wait. Bang! The juicer self-destructs – it sounds like a gunshot.)

MRS. MEREDITH. What the hell!

*(**MARY** enters. She has carrot juice on her face.)*

MARY. Not a problem–. The juicer kind of–. Need–. Right back.

*(**MARY** runs into the kitchen.)*

MRS. MEREDITH. Dick–.

DICK. Please, Richard.

MRS. MEREDITH. *(fake peasantries)* I want to inform you, *Dick*, that although I've only known you for what? Two minutes. I find you to be a most egregious young man and the thought of you having intercourse with my daughter, your, what would she be? Your common-law wife? Makes me want to–.

DICK. I just–.

MRS. MEREDITH. Please don't talk.

DICK. But–.

MRS. MEREDITH. I will now pray for your eternal soul, Dick.

*(**MRS. MEREDITH** bows her head in deep prayer. Pause. **DICK** waits.)*

DICK. I was just trying to…

> (**MRS. MEREDITH** *moves her lips when she prays. Beat.* **DICK** *begins to sing.*)

DICK. *(singing)*
> MRS. MEREDITH, YOU DO KNOW THAT PRAYER DOESN'T WORK
> SEVERAL-STUDIES-HAVE-SHOWN THAT PRAYER HAS NO PERKS
> DUKE UNIVERSITY WORKED WITH CHRISTIANS, MUSLIMS, AND BUDDHISTS TOO
> TO MAKE SURE THE STUDY WAS UNBIASED THEY THREW IN A JEW
> THE STUDY CONCLUDED THAT THEIR PRAYERS HAVE ZERO EFFECT
> ON THE PATIENT'S OUTCOME, THEY TOOK TIME TO TRIPLE CHECK

> (**MRS. MEREDITH** *prays harder.*)

DICK. *(singing)*
> ANOTHER STUDY DONE BY SIX MEDICAL CENTERS
> ALSO CONCLUDED THAT PRAYER HAD NO EFFECT WHATSOEVER
> IN FACT THE PATIENTS WHO WERE PRAYED FOR HAD MORE COMPLICATIONS
> THAN THOSE WHO RECEIVED NO PRAYERS OR VENERATIONS

> (**MRS. MEREDITH** *redoubles her efforts.*)

DICK. *(With jazz-hands he finishes the song.)*
> BOTH STUDIES WERE DOUBLE BLIND–.

MRS. MEREDITH. Get out!

DICK. I'm just trying–.

MRS. MEREDITH. Get out of my house you atheist bastard!

DICK. Actually I'm an agnostic who occasionally leans towards deism–.

MRS. MEREDITH. Get out, Dick!

> (**MARY** *enters holding half a glass of carrot juice.*)

MARY. What's going–!

MRS. MEREDITH. Oh my God!

MARY. Mom, what?

MRS. MEREDITH. My daughter is dating a communist!

MARY. He's not a communist; he's a freethinker.

MRS. MEREDITH. That's even worse!

(**MRS. MEREDITH** *exits.*)

MARY. What the hell–?

DICK. I was trying to have an honest–!

MARY. I warned you about being honest!

DICK. What should I talk about?

MARY. The weather! The weather is a wonderful thing to talk about!

DICK. You mean small–.

MARY. Yes! Polite, inane, meaningless small talk! That's what you do when you meet your future mother-in-law for the first time on Thanksgiving!

DICK. But that's all we ever do! No one really says anything substantive.

(*A far off gunshot – that stops them.*)

MARY. This is goodbye.

DICK. We can make this work.

MARY. There's a gunman on campus. And this is how you're going to spend your last minutes. Haranguing some poor pawn in human resources about the spot on her lung?

DICK. Brecht was right! People live in these little worlds. Watching meaningless romantic melodramas, and the corporate evening news. We need to wake up to reality!

(*She starts to leave.*)

DICK. Wait! I can do it. Small talk.

MARY. You're incapable.

DICK. One hundred percent small talk.

MARY. Prove it.

(Beat. He pulls himself together.)

DICK. ...It's...

MARY. Yes?

DICK. Raining.

MARY. ...Yes.

DICK. ...I heard it's going to rain tomorrow.

MARY. Really, cause I heard it's going to stop. I get regular weather updates on my iPhone.

DICK. You like your iPhone?

MARY. My whole life is in the palm of my hand.

DICK. Can you update your Facebook page from your iPhone–. I can't!

MARY. I knew it!

(She starts out.)

DICK. Mary wait!

(She pauses.)

Look...I'm about to be blown away in a meaningless act of violence. I just need you to know that I loved you.

*(Beat. **MARY** walks up and gives him a tender kiss on the cheek.)*

MARY. I have to practice.

*(She exits. Loud Rock and Roll – the lights back to the exit interview. **DICK** puts on his leg cast. The sign dances to life. It reads:)*

An Agnostic In A Foxhole

*(**DICK** sits back with his eyes closed. **EUNICE** sits on her desk with her collage.)*

EUNICE. *(dreamy)* Now imagine your own personal collage. What do you have pasted on it?

*(**CHLOE** runs in.)*

OFFSTAGE CHEERLEADERS. *(This cheer repeats as needed.)* Peanut Butter Reese's Cup mess with us I kick your butt!

EUNICE. Door!

CHLOE. The university's emergency alert system just–! A gunman was sighted in the Ronald Reagan Cafeteria! That's right next-door!

EUNICE. Where did you hear this?

CHLOE. The Campus Alert System on my iPhone.

EUNICE. Let me confirm.

(EUNICE professionally types on her laptop.)

DICK. A gunman?

CHLOE. *(nervous)* There may be more than one.

EUNICE. *(looking at her computer screen)* She is in fact correct. The police are on site. But, it says we should *(reading)* "stay where we are and take cover." Chloe, go to your office, get under your desk–.

CHLOE. Can't I stay here with–?

EUNICE. You have your own storage room.

CHLOE. But–.

EUNICE. And close the–.

CHLOE. But we got no locks.

EUNICE. Door!

CHLOE. Should I tell the cheerleader captain?

EUNICE. He'll figure it out. Save yourself.

(She exits.)

OFFSTAGE CHEERLEADERS. We're sexy and we're cute! We're feminine ta-boot! We're angry and we're tough! And we haven't had enough!

EUNICE. Door!

*(**CHLOE** runs back and closes the door. The **CHEERLEADERS** fade.)*

(nervous but professional) Shall we continue?

(EUNICE *calmly climbs under her desk.*)

DICK. But–.

EUNICE. *(from under her desk)* Next question–

DICK. You're going to interview me from under–.

EUNICE. Were you pleased with the university's health benefit plan?

DICK. Perhaps we should–.

EUNICE. The warning reads that we should stay put. They're worried that if we run some may end up a victim of friendly fire.

DICK. But–.

EUNICE. Do you want to be a victim of friendly fire?

DICK. Well no, but–.

EUNICE. Trust me, I had a workshop on exactly what to do in this situation. Were you pleased with the university's health benefit plan?

DICK. …That's a loaded question–.

(Rock and Roll. The sign boogies to life. It reads:)

Gravity Is Not Mad At You

(Outside the Ronald Reagan Cafeteria **WALTER** *starts to interview a Dean.)*

ACTOR #2 (WALTER). This is Walter Kendell, Fox News. And we are live nationwide. I'm here with Dean–.

STAGE MANAGER'S VOICE. Hold Please!

ACTOR #1. What?

STAGE MANAGER'S VOICE. The playwright has re-writes.
(From above, a silver platter is lowered from the fly system.* On it are new pages. The actors take them. The platter flies back up.)

ACTOR #2. Are you kidding me?

ACTOR #1. What is this?

---

* If your theatre doesn't have a fly system then perhaps the playwright's (or stage manager's) arm comes in from the side of the curtain, or proscenium arch, or perhaps the playwright runs out to the audience. Be creative.

STAGE MANAGER'S VOICE. Replacement scene. And he wants you to do it with German accents.

(The actors study the new lines for a moment.)

Go.

(The actors read the following scene, as they have not had time to rehearse it.)

(The sign boogies to life. It reads:)

The Alienation Effect

(The actors add thick German accents – they occasionally slip into German.)

ACTOR #1. *(reading to the audience)* Poet, playwright, and director Bertolt Brecht was born in Berlin on February 10th 1898 and died August 14th 1956.

ACTOR #2. Brecht thought that a theater should not be a place of *Amüsement** but a political lecture hall. Rather than sympathizing with the characters he encouraged his audience to be conscious thinking observers.

ACTOR #1. Brecht felt that the shattering of the theatrical illusion was critical.

ACTOR #2. Because when an audience loses themselves in a play they are not thinking.

ACTOR #2. If you become absorbed or *untertauchen*** in the entertainment then the theatre is nothing more than preparation for similar *untertauchen* in words and fantasies of theatrical leadership: like Herr Hitler.

ACTOR #1. Brecht deliberately set out to wake up his audience.

ACTOR #2. He called this "Verfremdungseffekt."

ACTOR #1. Sometimes called "The Alienation Effect."

ACTOR #2. And so in the interest of breaking the theatrical illusion we will now halt this play entitled *Die Ausgang Interviewen* and enact a totally different play.

ACTOR #1. A new play entitled: *Wenig Gespräch.*

---

* amusement

** immersed

ACTOR #2. Location:

ACTOR #1. A park bench. Not far from the University.

ACTOR #2. Characters:

ACTOR #1. Two *Mutters*.[*]

ACTOR #2. Time:

ACTOR #1. The Present.

(The sign lights up. It reads:)

Wenig Gespräch

(Underneath is the English translation:)

Small Talk

(Lights up on **BETH** *and* **SAMANTHA**, *two mothers with baby carriages. They sit on a park bench on a wonderful sunny day – sounds of birds chirping and children playing. They rock their carriages.)*

SAMANTHA. Looks like rain.

BETH. Yes, it does.

SAMANTHA. They say it's the rainiest December in ten years.

BETH. I believe it.

*(***BETH*** takes out a baby bottle.)*

SAMANTHA. Wait. You're not going to feed that to your child.

BETH. What?

SAMANTHA. Formula.

BETH. So?

SAMANTHA. It causes immune system shortfall and cell–culture contamination.

BETH. Does not.

SAMANTHA. Heard it on Fox and Friends.

BETH. I heard breastfeeding is the real problem.

SAMANTHA. No.

BETH. Breastfeeding causes thinning in the membranes of your vagina.

---

*mother

SAMANTHA. How do you know that?

BETH. *The View.*

SAMANTHA. Strange, I heard the problem was beef hormones – it also causes men's hair to fall out and teenage girls to grow abnormally large breasts.

BETH. How do you know–?

SAMANTHA. Oprah network.

BETH. Did you watch her "It's a New You" no-diet-diet show last week?

SAMANTHA. Missed it. What's the secret?

BETH. Salmon – At least three times a week.

SAMANTHA. I heard salmon has unacceptably high PCB contaminant levels.

BETH. Where?

SAMANTHA. CNN…or was it CNBC?

BETH. What difference does it make – Who can afford salmon today? Not in this economy.

SAMANTHA. Don't worry, things are going to get better next year.

BETH. How do you know?

SAMANTHA. ABC.

BETH. Cause Fox Business said there'll be another big downturn right after the holidays.

SAMANTHA. Oh, did you hear that our national debt is out of control – Every man, woman and child in America owes almost fifty thousand dollars to foreign countries?

BETH. I heard that debt isn't as important as debt-to-income ratio. Which, according to the experts, is just fine.

SAMANTHA. How do you–?

BETH. Rush Limbaugh prayed to God and got an answer.

SAMANTHA. PBS said there was no factual evidence proving the existence of God.

BETH. Really, cause I heard that science has now proven that God is really out there.

SAMANTHA. Where did you hear that?

BETH. *Science Friday,* maybe, or was it _____ *(fill in the name of a popular sitcom).*

SAMANTHA. That's not what they said on NPR. They said there's no way to prove God.

BETH. No, that's evolution. I watched a special the other night that said evolution was a hoax made up by homosexual scientists who hate God.

SAMANTHA. Dr. Laura told me that most scientists aren't religious.

BETH. God's Country Radio Network told me that science and religion have kissed and made up. They're all now in agreement that the world is six thousand years old.

SAMANTHA. I heard it was billions and billions of years old.

BETH. No. The creation was created in only six days.

SAMANTHA. How do you know that?

BETH. Heard it on a Billy Graham special–. *(thinking)* Or it might've been the Republican National Convention.

SAMANTHA. Strange cause I heard that it was all created in a single afternoon.

BETH. Huh.

SAMANTHA. Yeah. I heard that the great Father of All Spirits woke up the Sun Mother, who ventured into the dark caves where her internal heat melted the ice creating rivers, and streams, and the world as we know it.

BETH. How do you know that?

SAMANTHA. Not sure, might've been the Public Access Channel.

BETH. Cause I heard that God-the-Father-almighty-creator-of-heaven-and-earth-and-Jesus-Christ-his-only-Son-our-Lord-who-was-conceived-by-the-Holy-Spirit-born-of-the-Virgin-Mary-suffered-under-Pontius-Pilate-was-cruci-fied-died-and-was-buried-He-descended-into-hell-the-third-day-he-rose-again-from-the-dead-he-ascended-in-to-heaven-and-is-seated-at-the-right-hand-of-the-Father-from-thence-he-shall-come-to-judge-the-living-and-the-dead.

SAMANTHA. Huh. How do you know that?

BETH. *Wheel of Fortune. (beat)* Oh, I forgot to tell you. My little Sarah said the cutest thing. She said, Mommy did you know that a cheetah can run faster than any other animal on earth.

SAMANTHA. Huh. How does she know that?

BETH. Her teacher.

SAMANTHA. Cause my sweet little Sandy told me that there were new doubts about the cheetahs speed – they now think that antelopes may be faster for short distances.

BETH. How does she–?

SAMANTHA. *Animal Planet.*

BETH. That's not what my little Sarah said. Cheetahs are faster.

SAMANTHA. Huh.

BETH. Huh. Wonder who's right?

SAMANTHA. Yeah, wonder.

(Beat – they think.)

Suppose we could find out for ourselves?

BETH. How would we…?

SAMANTHA. Don't know.

(Beat – they think.)

BETH. I guess we'd have to go to Africa.

SAMANTHA. Probably so.

(Beat. They continue the following in deep thought.)

BETH. And find a healthy cheetah.

SAMANTHA. Right.

BETH. And an antelope.

SAMANTHA. And a car.

BETH. And then we'd have to get the cheetah and the antelope running.

SAMANTHA. Really, really fast.

BETH. It would be best not to get them running at the same time cause the cheetah would most likely get distracted and eat the antelope.

SAMANTHA. Right, separate tests would be best. And then once they're running we'd have to follow them in the car.

BETH. And we'd have to test to make sure the speedometer was properly calibrated.

SAMANTHA. Right.

SAMANTHA. And we'd have to get someone else to verify our results. You know, some sort of peer–review process.

SAMANTHA. Yes, peer–review would be important. *(beat)* And then we'd know.

BETH. You're right, then we'd know.

SAMANTHA. Huh.

BETH. Huh. What do ya know?

SAMANTHA. What do ya know?

(They sit there rocking their baby carriages as the lights fade.)

(Rock and Roll – the screen sputters to life. It reads:)

God Found Me A Parking Space

(**EUNICE** *hides under her desk.* **DICK** *beside it.*)

EUNICE. *(anxious)* It's quiet. I think we're going to be okay. We're safe. I know it.

DICK. How do you–?

EUNICE. God has blessed me with all these annoying little complications cause it's all in his plan.

DICK. You mean like day-to-day...

EUNICE. Yes, a plan for everything. When I arrived at work this morning, it was pouring, and a parking spot opened up right in front of the building. And I said thank you Jesus.

DICK. Does a parking spot open up for you every time it rains?

EUNICE. No, sometimes I have to park in the student lot.

DICK. That's at least a twenty-minute–.

EUNICE. And on those days I say, thank you Jesus.

DICK. But it's a twenty-minute–

EUNICE. And that's okay cause I know that by making me walk in the rain, my Lord is trying to teach me patience.

DICK. How do you–?

EUNICE. Why else would he make me walk so far?

DICK. Perhaps he thinks you need a little exercise.

EUNICE. Patience *and* exercise.

DICK. My car wouldn't start this morning, what does that–?

EUNICE. When my car doesn't start it's because Jesus wants to remind me about the importance of maintenance.

DICK. And when it runs well?

EUNICE. He wants me to enjoy the smooth road to heaven.

DICK. How about a flat tire?

EUNICE. Jesus wants to tell me not to take things for granted.

DICK. Oil change?

EUNICE. We must renew our vows and throw out the dark part of our soul.

DICK. You believe that. You actually–.

EUNICE. Absolutely.

DICK. You might be the one to answer a question for me.

EUNICE. If I can.

DICK. My girlfriend, ex-girlfriend, was an aspiring oboist.

EUNICE. So you mentioned.

DICK. She practiced sometimes eight-ten hours a day. Within weeks after we started dating she developed O.S. – Overuse Syndrome – a pain in her third and fourth fingers making it impossible to practice. What does that mean?

EUNICE. It's God's way of telling her that she needs to stop obsessing and give the glory of her music to him.

DICK. Not playing kind of depressed her and so doctors prescribed a series of anti-depressants, which brought on suicidal thoughts. What does–.

EUNICE. God wants you to know that only he can heal.

DICK. So I took her on vacation to Yellowstone, which brought on even greater depression. Helping her to her feet, after she tried to jump to her death, I twisted a testicle. The ambulance taking both of us to the hospital collided with a moose – I'm not making this up – this massive moose, which untwisted my testicle but then a small lump was discovered during a scrotal ultrasound. After surgery it was called benign.

EUNICE. God is letting you know that you need to sit back and reevaluate your life.

DICK. By giving me a twisted–?

EUNICE. He wants to teach you that sometimes love hurts.

DICK. The doctors ordered me to abstain from sex for three months. During the hiatus my girlfriend gets pregnant, i.e. not mine.

EUNICE. God is questioning your impropriety.

DICK. We broke up. After giving birth to little Ben, her Overuse Syndrome clears up and she wants to get back together. I forgive her fling with her Gestalt Therapist. But the next day she gets a call inviting her to audition for the National Symphony Orchestra in Washington DC, and so she breaks up with me again because she's convinced that her fingers will stop working if she has anything to do with me. What was God's plan in that?

EUNICE. He wants you to abstain from sex–.

DICK. Couldn't he just tell me that! Couldn't he just write in the clouds, "Hi, Dick, I just twisted and untwisted your balls so that you will abstain until you marry. Signed God." Wouldn't that be more effective?

EUNICE. God doesn't work that way. Writing in clouds lacks sophistication.

DICK. And twisting testicles does?

EUNICE. You can't see the big picture. If you could you'd know that everything will work out for the best in the end.

DICK. Not for the moose. It didn't die quietly. They had to take us out of the damaged ambulance and wait for another. While we're laying there on the gurneys, just a few feet away, this big moose is moaning and flopping around. So the ambulance driver decides to put it out of its misery – he takes a tire iron from the ambulance and begins beating the moose! Do you realize how long it takes to beat a moose to death!

EUNICE. God wants you to know that what he gives he can take away.

DICK. The driver was so preoccupied with whacking the moose that he forgot to put the ambulance in park. It rolls back over us. Breaking my girlfriends arm and severing my foot. Doctors reattach it in a fifteen–hour operation. What does that–.

EUNICE. He has a bigger plan! You just don't see it!

DICK. How do you know that you're correctly reading the mind of God?

EUNICE. I'm confident in what God has assigned me.

DICK. But what if the overuse syndrome means that God finds the sound of oboes annoying? And what about the dead moose – the fact that it took so long to die – Does it mean that moose are evil beings in God's eyes? And the topper has got to be the broken arm and severed foot. Why is it that people pray for miracles all the time and they, according to you, come true? The spot on your lung. But that same God never answers the prayers of amputees? Their limbs never grow back.

EUNICE. Yours–.

DICK. Because of Science! For thousands of years amputees' prayers went unanswered! What does that mean? Does God hate amputees?!

(A gunshot – closer. They are quiet – scared.)

EUNICE. Oh my God, I think that was in the building.

DICK. *(whispering)* And what is God's purpose now?

EUNICE. God wants us to realize how precious life is.

DICK. By killing us?

EUNICE. I don't believe I'm going to be killed!

DICK. But *if* we are?

EUNICE. Then God must need me up in heaven for some reason!

DICK. If God needs us in heaven–.

EUNICE. I didn't say *us*, I said *me!*

DICK. If God needs *you* in heaven why doesn't he just have you die peacefully in your sleep? Why make a big show of it! Why do it in such a way that someone might doubt–?

EUNICE. I'm not a religious expert!

DICK. You came up with a pretty good reason for the tragic bludgeoning of a moose; I think that qualifies you as an expert!

EUNICE. All I know is that God is testing me.

(a gunshot)

DICK. Shit. That one was closer.

EUNICE. *(terrified)* God is testing me.

(another gunshot a little closer)

(crying) God is testing me.

(another gunshot a little closer)

(starting to panic) God is testing me. God is testing me. God is testing me.

(Gunshot. Blackout. Silence.)

(In the darkness the screen fades up. It reads:)

Intermission

ACT TWO

(The sign twinkles to life – It reads:)

Towards A Poor Theatre

(The effervescent **CHEERLEADERS** *run center – they are once again followed by the ski-masked* **GUNMAN** *who stands quietly in the background.)*

CHEERLEADER #1. *(spirited)* Welllll–come back!

CHEERLEADER #2. *(bubbly)* Yeaaaa!

(They chest bump.)

CHEERLEADER #1. We hope you had a fantastic intermission! Before we begin act two–!

CHEERLEADER #2. Yea, Act Two!

CHEERLEADER #1. Brief announcements!

CHEERLEADER #2. Did you know the theatre is poor?

CHEERLEADER #1. Currently your typical non-profit theatre receives only fifty percent of its operating budget from ticket sales!

CHEERLEADER #2. Yea, ticket sales!

CHEERLEADER #1. The rest comes from grants!

CHEERLEADER #2. Donations!

CHEERLEADER #1. Local businesses!

CHEERLEADER #2. Yea! Local businesses!

CHEERLEADER #1. And patrons like you!

CHEERLEADER #2. Goooooooo patrons!

CHEERLEADER #1. If you don't help your local theatre you could lose it!

CHEERLEADER #2. Just a few bucks really makes a difference!

CHEERLEADER #1. And don't think that the NEA–!

CHEERLEADER #2. National Endowment for the Arts!

CHEERLEADER #1. –is going to help 'cause it's funding has been drastically cut 'cause of attacks by people like Senator Jesse Helms of North Carolina!

CHEERLEADER #2. He forced through congress a law that reads, in part…!

CHEERLEADER #1. Grants from the National Endowment for the Arts must take into consideration the general standards of *decency and respect* for the diverse beliefs and values of the American public!

CHEERLEADER #2. This play doesn't qualify!

CHEERLEADER #1. *(really upbeat)* And Senator Jesse Helms is dead!!!!

BOTH. *(shaking their pom poms)* Yeeeeeeeea!

CHEERLEADER #1. But this theatre has found a new way to make ends meet!

CHEERLEADER #2. It's true!

CHEERLEADER #1. So for act two we'll be selling commercial time. Now and then we'll be interrupting the action of the play to sell you crap you don't need!

CHEERLEADER #2. Yea, crap!

CHEERLEADER #1. We figure you put up with this shit when you watch TV and product placement during Hollywood movies!

CHEERLEADER #2. Don't forget pop up windows on the web!

CHEERLEADER #1. So why shouldn't the theatre grow up and face reality!

CHEERLEADER #2. Yea, Reality!

CHEERLEADER #1. It totally makes sense!

CHEERLEADER #2. It totally does!

CHEERLEADER #1. So please enjoy act two with just a few words from our sponsors!

CHEERLEADER #2. Are we done?

CHEERLEADER #1. Totally! Ready? Hit it! Give me a "C!"

AUDIENCE. "C!"

CHEERLEADER #2. Commercial interruptions!

CHEERLEADER #1. Give me a "P!"

AUDIENCE. "P!"

CHEERLEADER #2. Product placement!

CHEERLEADER #1. Give me an "N!"

AUDIENCE. "N!"

CHEERLEADER #2. No National Endowment for the Arts funding!

CHEERLEADER #1. Give me a "J!"

AUDIENCE. "J!"

CHEERLEADER #2. Jesse Helms!

CHEERLEADER #1. Give me a "D!"

AUDIENCE. "D!"

CHEERLEADER #2. Is dead!

CHEERLEADER #1. What's it spell?!

CHEERLEADER #2. Ah...still got nuthin'!

CHEERLEADER #1. Go theatre!

CHEERLEADER #2. Enjoy the show!

BOTH. *(shaking their pom poms)* Yeeeeeeeea!

(The **GUNMAN** *points his gun at the* **CHEERLEADERS** *and escorts them offstage.)*

(After they exit we hear **CHEERLEADER #1** *scream.)*

CHEERLEADER #1. *(screaming – offstage)* No! No!

(gunshot)

CHEERLEADER #2. *(screaming – offstage)* No. Please! For the love of God!

(A second gunshot. Silence. No Rock and Roll this time – the screen flickers to life. It reads:)

What's It Like To Kiss A Girl?

(The lights come up on **DICK** *and his wrapped foot hiding beside the desk,* **EUNICE** *cowers under it. The scene is as it was before only now there is a Diet Coke sitting on the desk.)*

DICK. *(quietly – on the office phone)* We are in a storage room on the third floor...yes, Officer...thank you. *(hangs up)* They think they have the gunman cornered in the cheerleaders practice room on the first floor. They want us to stay where we are.

EUNICE. *(whispering)* He's answered my prayers! *(weeping with joy)* I know...I know you, God...I know that you are omniscient and omnipotent and omnibenevolent.

DICK. Then why is there evil?

EUNICE. Cause he can't prevent it.

DICK. Then he's not omnipotent.

EUNICE. He allows evil cause he's testing our character.

DICK. If he is omniscient then he already knows the test results.

EUNICE. He tests us because he loves us.

DICK. An omnibenevolent being allows crap like this? How is that love?

EUNICE. God allows evil so that you'll enjoy the good things in life. If you never knew thirst you'd never experience the joy of a cool drink.

DICK. God wanted me to enjoy the day, so he scared the living shit out of me. That makes total sense. You know, I think I might've peed myself a little.

(Several gunshots come from the first floor.)

EUNICE. *(panicking)* Then there is only one answer–. *(beat)* We're being punished.

DICK. For what?

EUNICE. I don't know...Homosexual marriage?

DICK. God has sent a crazed gunman into the building to–!

EUNICE. He knows. He knows what I've done.

DICK. You're married to a–?

EUNICE. No. But I've had...thoughts. Of late, I've been looking at...Chloe.

DICK. Chloe?

EUNICE. My work-study. Nothing major, just little day-dreams.

DICK. I really don't want to hear–.

EUNICE. I don't know where these thoughts come from–.

DICK. It's nothing…Human nature. Everyone does it.

EUNICE. Good people don't.

DICK. Yes they do. So what, you lusted after a woman–.

EUNICE. I didn't *lust!*

DICK. Shhhh.

EUNICE. I just wondered what it might be like to give her…a…a quick little kiss on the lips.

DICK. Did your thoughts hurt anyone?

EUNICE. I've offended God!

DICK. You are telling me that in this vast universe, that because you used your imagination and fantasized–.

EUNICE. I didn't fantasize! I…I…had an innocent little daydream.

DICK. It's *that* important to God?

EUNICE. It must be.

DICK. Do you realize how narcissistic that is?

EUNICE. Is not.

DICK. That's the definition of narcissistic.

EUNICE. Then you tell me. Why is this happening?

DICK. I don't know. Maybe it's because we live in an anxiety filled society where we blindly accept a bunch of arbitrary rules rather than thinking things through for ourselves–.

(**EUNICE**'s *cell rings with* What a Friend We Have In Jesus. *She grabs it.*)

EUNICE. It's a text. *(reading it)* It's the police…It wasn't the gunman they cornered downstairs. It was the school mascot. They don't know where the gunman is–. *(closing her cell)* We must pray. God wants us to pray.

DICK. I'm not the praying type–.

EUNICE. You must pray! Now!

DICK. We must be quiet.

EUNICE. If you don't pray we'll die!

(**EUNICE** *prays.* **DICK** *can't.*)

(*A holy sound of a harp. The sign reads:*)

Imagine Every Little Snowflake

(*In a special light A* **PRIEST** *walks into the scene. If possible he should be decked out in full regalia.* **EUNICE** *does not see the* **PRIEST**.)

PRIEST. Go on, Dick, pray with her.

DICK. Father McCarthy, what are you...?

PRIEST. You obviously are beginning to see that the end is coming and you're replaying your life. In particular that day you lost your faith.

DICK. Father, I have so many questions. How could an omniscient, omnipotent–.

PRIEST. You're making such a fuss. All right, we'll go over it one more time. Ready? The Son is the same age as his Father, and although the Holy Ghost proceeded from the Father and Son, it too is equal to them; that is to say, it too is of the same age as the other two–.

DICK. But Father–.

PRIEST. According to celestial mathematics one times three equals three, and three times one equals one, and if we take two from three? We are left with three. And if we add one to one to one we get?

DICK. Ah...

PRIEST. One. Think of it as Me, Myself and I–. Although that analogy has not been approved by the Ecumenical Council, it does make a lot of sense – even though it's the wrong way to think of it. And so if I asked you what two plus one, minus two, plus three, minus one is, you'd answer?

DICK. ...Ah...one?

PRIEST. That's right! Although I'd've also accepted the answer "Three." Let us pray.

(*The* **PRIEST** *prays.*)

DICK. Father, you do know that there have been several studies that show that prayer doesn't–.

(The PRIEST *breaks into song.)*

PRIEST. *(half chanting, half singing)*
> A THING ISN'T NECESSARILY UNTRUE JUST BECAUSE WE DON'T UNDERSTAND IT.

DICK. But it also isn't necessarily true just because it's ancient or revered.

PRIEST. *(chanting/singing)*
> YOU CANNOT EXPLAIN EVERYTHING AND THAT WHICH YOU CANNOT EXPLAIN IS GOD.

DICK. But that means that God must be getting smaller and smaller because science keeps explaining more and more.

PRIEST. *(chanting/singing)*
> SCIENCE AND RELIGION ARE TOTALLY COMPATIBLE.

DICK. Where did you hear that?

PRIEST. *(chanting/singing)*
> I THINK IT WAS *FOX AND FRIENDS*.

DICK. Why can't we just think things through for our self–.

PRIEST. Because the world is too complicated and we are sinful, wretched, scum–. Is that a Diet Coke?

DICK. What?

PRIEST. You know forgiving the flock really takes it out of you – I could use a little refreshment.

DICK. Sure. Help yourself.

*(**DICK** grabs the Diet Coke and gives it to the **PRIEST**. He takes a drink.)*

PRIEST. Ahh. That sure is good.

DICK. Father–.

PRIEST. Imagine the Mona Lisa. Can you do that, Dick? Got her firmly in your head?

DICK. ...Sure.

PRIEST. Now take a tiny bit of her – nothing bigger than this can. If this was all you knew of the Mona Lisa what would you know?

DICK. Not much?

PRIEST. Exactly! You wouldn't see the big picture. This little can is your life. You must believe that maybe, if you're not naughty but nice, God will let you see the big picture. But for now you must be satisfied with only this. And it sure is satisfying.

DICK. But why? I mean, people being satisfied with that is what caused our problems. We shouldn't be satisfied. We should be striving for more. More understanding. More cures. More–.

PRIEST. What was it? Why did you lose your faith, Dick?

DICK. I prefer Richard.

PRIEST. You were such a pretty altar boy. What caused the sin of ambiguity and doubt to rear its ugly head?

DICK. ...It was the summer after I graduated from college – I met this girl.

PRIEST. A woman – knew it!

DICK. An archeology student. She invited me to go on a dig in Egypt. We joined a group of archeologists who had been searching for years trying to find evidence of Moses and the millions of Jews who, according to the Bible, wandered the desert for 40 years. You'd think they'd leave something behind. Fire pits, graves, campsites, latrines, maybe even a little petrified manna – something. A million hours of archaeological excavation and the most advanced equipment found nothing. That's when I began to doubt. Several million people wandering the desert for forty years and no archeological evidence?

PRIEST. Have you ever met a Jew? Very clean people.

(Gunshot – a little closer. **EUNICE** *whimpers.)*

PRIEST. There's little time left. Are you going to join us in prayer or not?

DICK. Studies have shown–.

PRIEST. *(chanting/singing)*
THEN I MUST ASK YOU TO IMAGINE EVERY LITTLE
    SNOWFLAKE THAT'S EVER DRIFTED FROM THE SKY.
(speaking) Can you do that?

DICK. ...I guess.

PRIEST. *(chanting/singing)*
> AND NOW ADD TO IT EVERY BRIGHT AUTUMN LEAF THAT
> HAS EVER DRIFTED TO EARTH.

DICK. *(confused)* …Okay.

PRIEST. *(chanting/singing)*
> ADD TO IT EVERY GRAIN OF SAND ON EVERY BEACH IN THE
> WORLD.

DICK. I don't know where you're going with this, but okay.

PRIEST. *(chanting/singing)*
> AND NOW MULTIPLY THAT BY THE TOTAL NUMBER OF
> RAINDROPS THAT HAVE FALLEN FROM HEAVEN SINCE
> THE BEGINNING OF TIME.
>
> *(speaking)* What does that add up to?

DICK. …A lot?

PRIEST. That's right, a lot. That number, that vast number, is less than the total number of years you will burn in hell if you don't repent.

DICK. For what?

PRIEST. *(singing with jazz-hands)*
> FOR DOUBTING GOD'S LOVE.

> *(a gunshot)*

Goodbye, Dick. I shall pray for you.

DICK. Wait!

> *(The lights begin to fade on the* **PRIEST.***)*

PRIEST. Just remember – one times three equals three, and three times one equals one, and if we take two from three? We are left with…we are left with…we are left with…

> *(Another holy harp and the* **PRIEST** *and his Diet Coke fade.)*

DICK. Father?

> *(A gunshot down the hall.* **EUNICE** *screams.)*

We must be quiet!

> *(The phone on Eunice's desk rings.* **DICK** *dives for it.)*
>
> *(whispering)* Hello.

(Upbeat newscast music. The sign dances and sparkles. It reads:)

Fox News Alert

Brought To You By

[Corporate Logo 1]

[Corporate Slogan 1]*

(In a separate light we find **WALTER** *from Fox News. Beside him stands* **MARY**, *with her iPhone and oboe case. Her arm is back in the sling.* **WALTER** *speaks into a microphone – it's a live broadcast.)*

WALTER. Am I speaking to Dick Fig?

DICK. *(whispering)* Richard.

WALTER. This is Walter Kendell, Fox News. And we are live nationwide.

DICK. *(whispering)* Can't talk.

WALTER. Got your girlfriend here.

DICK. Mary?

WALTER. With her help we've found you. But first can you give us an update – Where's the gunman?

DICK. *(whispering)* In the building someplace, don't know.

WALTER. If you were to survive what do you think God's purpose for you is–?

DICK. Can I talk to–.

WALTER. Can you describe the terror you're feeling–?

DICK. May I please talk to her–!

WALTER. Sure, just remember we're live!

*(***WALTER*** holds the microphone in front of ***MARY***.)*

MARY. *(in tears – out to the camera)* Richard?

DICK. Mary. I'm so sorry.

MARY. So am I.

---

* Here, the sign projects commonly recognized coporate logos, followed by their respective slogans (e.g. companies like Ford, Dell, and Pantene have been used in past productions). If your theatre finds local businesses or organizations that would like to buy this or one of the following advertisements, please change the sign to accommodate.

DICK. I should've tried harder.

MARY. Me too.

DICK. More and more I see the absurdity of it – I was jealous of an oboe. Can you imagine such a thing?

MARY. Yes, I lived it.

DICK. That nice wood oboe you had–.

MARY. The Crampon Professional Model 3613?

DICK. Yes. There's something I need to tell you…it wasn't stolen from the back of my car. In fact…I broke it. One day I just went nuts and drove over it with my car… *(quiet/desperate)* More and more I'm convinced that jealousy is the weakest and perhaps most destructive of human emotions. Back in catechism class when they said that God was "jealous", I knew it couldn't be the real God they were talking about – no perfect being could ever feel such a base, stupid, human emotion. They're simply projecting their hopes on to the empty universe–.

MARY. Hold on a sec…I need to wrap my head around this…You drove your Prius over my Crampon Professional Model 3613?

DICK. Yes, but now I realize that we, not God, create our purpose. Yours is the oboe. You're one of the lucky ones, you were a little obsessive about it, but you found it – so many people live their lives and never find a purpose, never even look, worse, live their lives with a secondhand purpose they borrowed from their parents, their religion, but never owned. I just hope someday you'll find room in your heart for something else too – another human being to share life with. And as for little Ben–.

MARY. Oh crap! Ben. *(to* **WALTER***)* Where did I leave the kid?

WALTER. You had it when we–.

MARY. Oh crap.

   *(***MARY*** runs off.)*

WALTER. Dick, can you tell me about the terror you feel in eight seconds or less? *(pressing his finger to his ear-mic)* Hold on…this just in – the location of the gunman is unknown. The police want everyone in the building not to move. They don't want what happened to the team mascot to happen to anyone else. Dick, how does that make you feel?

DICK. How do you think? Like shit.

WALTER. Please be aware of FCC language restrictions. Hold on–. *(He presses a finger to his ear-mic.)* So sorry, gotta cut away. *(upbeat – to the audience)* Right back after this.

(Upbeat newscast music. The sign dances and sparkles. It reads:)

I'm Confident Cause I'm Comfortable

(A spotlight on a pretty businesswoman holding a briefcase and wearing only a bra from the waist up.)

BUSINESSWOMAN IN A BRA. Did you ever get the feeling that other women are having more fun than you? They are! That's cause they're wearing the right bra.

*(Two handsome **BUSINESSMEN** also holding briefcases join her.)*

BUSINESSMAN #1. Did you know that eight out of ten women are wearing the wrong size?

BUSINESSMAN #2 *(WALTER)*. An ill–fitting bra can cause back pain, tingling in the arms–.

BUSINESSMAN #1. Restricted breathing, abrasions, rashes–.

BUSINESSMAN #2 (**WALTER**). Even chronic headaches.

BUSINESSWOMAN IN A BRA. So don't be a victim and while you're at it crack that glass ceiling. Let the friendly experts at the Bra Store fit you the way nature intended. The Bra Store.

*(The **BUSINESSMEN** smile at her. She flirtatiously grins back.)*

BUSINESSWOMAN IN A BRA. I'm confident cause I'm comfortable.

(A scream offstage. Gunshot. The lights jump back to the office. The sign boogies. It reads:)

The End Is Near

Brought To You By

[Corporate Logo 2]

[Corporate Slogan 2]

*(Gunshot! That one was close. **EUNICE** screams. **DICK** stifles her.)*

DICK. *(whispering)* We must be–. Completely–. Quiet.

(He slowly takes his hand from her mouth.)

EUNICE. *(weeping)* That last one…I think it was Chloe.

*(Lights up on **WALTER**.)*

WALTER. Dick? Can you hear me?

*(For a second **DICK** can't figure out where **WALTER**'s voice is coming from and then he realizes that he's still holding the phone.)*

DICK. *(whispering into the phone)* Can't talk.

WALTER. Hold on. *(pressing his finger to his ear-mic)* …Mr. Fig, I've just received word that the police are right down the hall. And you should make no sudden movements.

*(**MARY** runs in pushing the baby carriage.)*

MARY. Found it!

WALTER. And now this Fox News Alert!

(The sign boogies. It reads:)

A Car Chase In San Bernardino

Brought To You By

[Corporate Logo 3]

[Corporate Slogan 3]

*(In a pool of light a **LADY NEWSCASTER**.)*

LADY NEWSCASTER. Walter, our thoughts and prayers go out to those poor trapped people and their families. But first we want everyone to know that we are also keeping an eye on a car chase in San Bernardino. And in other news All Star pitcher Hank Starling was asked how he's doing after being hit in that freak accident during the opening game of the year.

(In a pool of light we see **HANK STARLING,** *a professional baseball player holding a baseball bat. His eye is heavily bandaged.)*

HANK STARLING. *(He has trouble concentrating.)* I hope to be back soon, but I don't know when. All I know is that God works in mysterious ways. Oh, and I forgive the president for the wild pitch.

(He kisses his fist and points toward heaven – lights out on **HANK STARLING.** *The* **LADY NEWSCASTER** *continues.)*

LADY NEWSCASTER. Later tonight I'll be interviewing Hank about his mother's Alzheimer's and how it brought them closer together. That's at eight, right before the new Fox reality show *Church Swap.* This week members of the St. Peter's Episcopal Church of Whitehead, New Hampshire will switch places with members of the New Birth Missionary Pentecostal Church of Birmingham Alabama. If you love snakes you won't want to miss this. And now back to "Gunman Drama – The fight for life!" But first this…

(Lights out on the **LADY NEWSCASTER** *– the sign jumps to life. It reads:)*

Leave Her Guessing

(A spotlight on **BUSINESSWOMAN #2** *holding a briefcase – She is fully clothed.)*

BUSINESSWOMAN #2. I always can't help but wonder – is he wearing…

*(***BUSINESSMAN #1** *steps up beside her. He carries a briefcase. He pulls down his pants – He wears boxers.)*

BUSINESSMAN #1. Boxers?

BUSINESSWOMAN #2. Or?

(**BUSINESSMAN #2** *steps up beside her. He also carries a briefcase. He pulls down his pants – He is wearing briefs.*)

BUSINESSMAN #2 (**WALTER**). Or briefs?

BUSINESSMAN #1. One size doesn't fit all.

BUSINESSWOMAN #2. And it's important to get the right size.

(**BUSINESSWOMAN #2** *smiles at them. They smile back.*)

BUSINESSWOMAN #2. The Underwear Store.

(*Black out. The sign jumps to life. It reads:*)

God Ate My Homework

Brought To You By

[Corporate Logo 4]

[Corporate Slogan 4]

(*The office. Pause. Silence.*)

DICK. It's quiet. Too quiet.

(*The lights fade up on the ski-masked* **GUNMAN** *quietly standing behind him.*)

EUNICE. Think it's over? Maybe that last shot was the bastard killing himself? I think he did. I think the bastard killed himself.

(*The* **GUNMAN** *walks into their sight.* **EUNICE** *screams. The* **GUNMAN** *points the gun at her.*)

EUNICE. Please...please...wait...

(*During the following the* **GUNMAN** *does not react. He simply points the gun at her.*)

(*terrified – weeping – rambling*) Did...did...did you know that God loves you? ...Tell me that you know. Someplace...down in your heart you know...but you have to ask for his forgiveness...with all your heart... And then...and then...you'll go to heaven. (*beat*) Would you like to see my collage?

(Weeping, EUNICE holds up her hopes and dreams collage.)

EUNICE. *(cont.) (pointing to various pictures on the collage)* These are my dreams. …This one…this one is the chlorine–free office I'm going to have some day. And this is where I'm going to travel once I become fluent in… in…I forgot…and this represents the weight I'm going to lose…and this is my book about…forgiveness…

(The masked GUNMAN is unmoved.)

(angry – sobbing) Say something! (Beat) Fine. You know what–. Maybe that's the problem. Too much damn forgiveness! Maybe what we need is a little bit of goddamn guilt around here! Maybe we need to hold ourselves accountable! …Forgiveness just allows us to shit on each other and be forgiven and then shit on each other again!

(The GUNMAN takes pointblank aim.)

(more tears – shaking with fear) No. Please. I admit it. I don't know if there's a God. We…would rather guess than learn. Would rather have faith than deal with reality! We…we don't want to admit that it's just a road… with no priceless treasure at the end. *(calming)* A road that disappears over the horizon. And one day we finish our short section and the horizon is…it's just as far away as when we started.

DICK. If I may interject–.

EUNICE. I'm handling this! Trust me, I had a workshop! *(to the GUNMAN – gaining confidence)* It's so…so…evident that no divine security cameras are watching… And all the stars and planets and moons and rocks in the universe don't give a flying crap about us! *(laughing through her tears)* So it's time, it's time that we stop complaining about what ought to be and start taking responsibility for what *is!* It's time we stop saying God is in charge. Because he's doing a pretty shitty job! No one is in charge but us!

(The GUNMAN cocks the gun. She closes her eyes and waits for the shot.)

(He pulls the trigger. Click. The gun jams. He quickly cocks it again. Click, again. He struggles to fix it.)

EUNICE. *(tears of joy)* Ha! I take it all back! There *is* a God!

*(Taking advantage of the moment, **EUNICE** joyously runs for the door.)*

And he loves me! God loves me!

*(**EUNICE** runs back.)*

Forgot my collage! There is a God!

*(**EUNICE** runs out laughing.)*

*(A second later we hear massive gunfire as the police open up on **EUNICE** in the hall. If possible bits and pieces of her bullet riddled collage should fly in from the hallway.)*

(Dead silence. Far off a garbled police radio laments their mistake.)

*(Meanwhile the **GUNMAN** has fixed the gun and points it at **DICK**. The sign sparkles to life. It reads:)*

Salman Rushdie Eats A Ham Sandwich

*(**ACTOR #1** appears as Salman Rushdie, while **ACTRESS #1** holds a ham sandwich.)*

ACTOR #1 (SALMAN RUSHDIE). I will now–.

STAGE MANAGER'S VOICE. Hold Please!

ACTRESS #1. What now?

STAGE MANAGER'S VOICE. The playwright has more re-writes.

(From above a silver platter is lowered from the fly system.* On it are new pages. The actors take them. The platter flies back up.)

ACTOR #2. No rehearsal?

STAGE MANAGER'S VOICE. Do what you can.

*(The sign fades to: **The Alienation Effect – Part II**)*

---

* Once again, if your theatre doesn't have a fly system, come up with a cool, creative answer.

(Once again they must feel their way with bad German accents and no rehearsal.)

ACTOR #1. *(reading from the script)* German poet, playwright, and director Bertolt Brecht once said, "Art is not a mirror held up to reality, but a *Arbeitsgerät mit einem harten Kopfteil** with which to shape it."

ACTRESS #1. And so we will now–.

ACTOR #1. Put on a completely different play!

ACTRESS #1. So that you might not directly relate to the action but think about how it might apply to your life.

ACTOR #1. Now we halt this play entitled *Die Ausgang Interviewen.*

ACTRESS #1. And replace it with a play entitled *Wissenschaft im Gegensatz zu Religion.*

(The sign jumps to life. It reads:)

Wissenschaft im Gegensatz zu Religion

(Science vs. Religion.)

(As the actors take their places we hear a professional **C–SPAN ANNOUNCER.***)*

C–SPAN ANNOUNCER (V.O.). *(recorded)* And now on C–SPAN 2 a panel discussion during a meeting of the International Society for Science and Religion.

(Fade up on a conference. On one side sit two scientists, on the other two religious leaders.)

To the left you will find Dr. James Jaeger who holds a Chair at The Institute for Neurodegenerative Diseases at the University of California San Francisco.

*(***DR. JAEGER** waves at the audience.)*

And next to him Dr. Amy Katts, president of The Scientific Advisory Board and a distinguished profes-sor of Pathology at the Case Western University School of Medicine.

*(***DR. KATTS** waves at the audience.)*

Who would like to go first?

---

* hammer

DR. JAEGER. If I may? I have an important announcement. I'd like to announce that researchers at the University of California San Francisco have discovered a protein that reduces everything from Seasonal Affective Disorder to neural degeneration. This new protein, the H5–.

DR. KATTS. So sorry, Dr. Jaeger, I hate to interrupt, but we at Case Western are doing similar research and I believe that you might've made a small mistake.

DR. JAEGER. I don't think so.

DR. KATTS. The evidence is overwhelming that it's the H3 protein, not the H5, which is in fact the catalyst.

DR. JAEGER. I have the truth right here in this book – published by the University of California San Francisco Press.

(**DR. JAEGER** *holds up a scientific book.*)

DR. KATTS. That's not the right book. Here's the correct book – it's published by Case Western Press, limited.

(**DR. KATTS** *holds up a different scientific book.*)

DR. JAEGER. I don't know how to say this, but right-minded scientists don't believe in such nonsense.

DR. KATTS. Oh really. The miscoding of proteins often causes neurodegeneration–.

DR. JAEGER. Thank you for pointing out the obvious.

DR KATTS. But anyone who doesn't believe in the H3 protein is obviously blind to their own personal agenda.

DR. JAEGER. My agenda is to find truth.

DR. KATTS. Then why do you hate science?

DR. JAEGER. Okay, let's stop right here. *(to the audience)* Anyone who believes that the H3 protein is the catalytic agent must believe that neurodegenerative diseases occur *after* the patient has already suffered neural damage. Such ideas are simply a war on scientific thought.

DR. KATTS. Your promotion of the H5 protein is nothing more than a radical agenda. What Albert Einstein called an "abomination." *(to the audience)* People, you will suffer horrible consequences if you believe in his H5 protein theory.

DR. JAEGER. Theory! What're you calling a theory!

DR. KATTS. *(to the audience)* Have you noticed how many earthquakes there are in the Bay Area? Ever wonder why? It's because of bad science at the University of California San Francisco.

DR. JAEGER. People, the scientists at Case Western University are promoting activist science.

DR. KATTS. It's time to call forth an army of scientists!

DR. JAEGER. People, we must take up the sword to defend science against the hypocrites. Be unyielding to them just as you must slaughter those who don't believe in gravity!

DR. KATTS. People, remember what Einstein said, "We cannot let science be scoffed at. Rise up and defend the one true Science."

DR. JAEGER. Einstein also said "I will cast terror into the hearts of those who disbelieve." Einstein is clearly ordering us to slay all the male scientists at Case Western, as well as all the female scientists, except those who are virgins, who Einstein has ordered us to have as our concubines.

DR. KATTS. You and all the idolaters' scientists at the University of California San Francisco will forever be held in an eternal dungeon of pain!

DR. JAEGER. I curse you in the name of science for you have excited the wrath of Einstein!

DR. KATTS. And from the dungeon of pain you will see your lab assistants stoned to death!

DR. JAEGER. We shall smite you and your laboratories!

DR. KATTS. And your graduate students will be cursed for seven generations – their names will be expunged from all scientific journals! And then will come the locusts.

DR. JAEGER. The what?

DR. KATTS. Nomadracis septemfasciata!*

DR. JAEGER. Oh, locusts.

DR. KATTS. They will consume your labs and Petri dishes!

DR. JAEGER. And for your sin of not believing in the H5 protein you will be forced to suffer menstruation and painful childbirth!

(**DR. KATTS** *and* **DR. JAEGER** *storm off.*)

C–SPAN ANNOUNCER (V.O.). Very interesting. Now, on the right you'll find Gordon Hubert, the President of the Church of Jesus Christ of Latter-day Saints, also known as the Mormons.

(**DR. HUBERT** *waves at the audience.*)

And beside him Bishop Martha Dobson, the president of the Lutheran World Federation. Dr. Dobson has a PhD in religious studies from Yale.

(**DR. DOBSON** *waves at the audience.*)

C–SPAN ANNOUNCER (V.O.). Who would like to go first?

DR. HUBERT. If I may? I also have an important announcement.

C–SPAN ANNOUNCER (V.O.). Everyone please welcome Dr. Huber.

DR. HUBERT. I'd like to announce that we have found the golden plates.

DR. DOBSON. What? You expect me to believe–?

DR. HUBERT. I don't expect you to believe anything. I have Joseph Smith's lost golden plates right here.

(**DR. HUBERT** *takes out several large, very heavy gold plates.*)

DR. HUBERT. We had them tested by several of the world's most prestigious independent laboratories including the Technical University of Munich, the Swiss Federal Institute of Technology, Hewlett-Packard, as well as labs at Yale and Princeton. I have the results right here.

---

* the scientific name for Locust

(He takes out a pile of scientific reports. **DR. DOBSON** *studies them and the golden plates.)*

DR. HUBERT. *(cont.)* Cryptographers and code breakers from the CIA, MI–5 and Mossad have studied the inscriptions and come to the same conclusion. And that is that Joseph Smith's translation of these plates, using his hat and "seer stone," is correct – word for word. In addition we now have proof from the American Association for the Advancement of Science, the Royal Astronomical Society and the International Society of Ethnobiology, to name just a few, that there is in fact a Mormon Celestial Kingdom. Plus, The Society for American Archaeology has found physical evidence that Jesus Christ did in fact appear in America and live with the Indians.

DR. DOBSON. *(rather stunned)* Ah…this is…inspired.

DR. HUBERT. We now think that truth doesn't need to be inspired. In fact the only time humans need inspiration to find truth is when they are trying to hide the truth.

DR. DOBSON. I…I don't know what to say. *(looking at the piles of evidence)* It all makes sense.

DR. HUBERT. We will be posting the findings on the World Wide Web so everyone can study and test for themselves.

DR. DOBSON. *(at a loss for words)* I…ah…

DR. HUBERT. Dr. Dobson, you wish to make a statement?

DR. DOBSON. I had prepared remarks, but in light of these overwhelming findings, I guess there is only one thing to say… *(beat – to the audience)* Lutheranism is cancelled.

(blackout)

(In the darkness the sign slowly fades up. Without theatrics it simply reads: **The Exit Interview***)*

(Lights up on the office.)

(The GUNMAN *pulls off his ski mask – it's a young, confused college kid. His eyes are swollen. Sadness consumes him.)*

(The GUNMAN *leans against the desk. Gun still held on* DICK.*)*

GUNMAN. *(disturbed – tears)* …Can…

DICK. *(terrified)* …Yes?

GUNMAN. …Can you…

DICK. What is it?

GUNMAN. *(after a deep breath)* Can you believe all this rain? *(beat)* …Heard we might have more…

DICK. …I…haven't checked…

GUNMAN. Might not clear up till next week.

DICK. Yes…we've…had a lot of rain…

GUNMAN. Rainy days…they kinda get me down. You?

DICK. …Obviously not as much as…

GUNMAN. My adviser over in student health says I suffer from Seasonal Affective Disorder. Was thinking of getting myself some of those, you know, special full spectrum lights.

DICK. …Sounds like a good idea.

GUNMAN. It's just that life is so–. Shit. It just hit me.

DICK. What?

GUNMAN. I forgot to update my Facebook page before I started shooting…

DICK. …Bummer…

GUNMAN. *(tears)* Sometimes it's just the little things, you know…went to the cafeteria this morning. Thought maybe some V8 juice would make me feel better. They advertise this a low-sodium V8. Doctors tell me I got high blood pressure so I should reduce my sodium intake. And then I read the side of the can – two hundred eighty milligrams of sodium. And that's the low sodium version! What the does regular V8 got – a fuckin' salt mine?

DICK. *(terrified)* …V8 juice is made with tomatoes.

GUNMAN. I like tomatoes.

DICK. They sure are good. But tomatoes naturally have salt…I think what they meant is…they didn't *add* any additional salt…

GUNMAN. *(wiping his tears)* Oh. That makes sense…they should put that on the side of the can…the cafeteria lady didn't have an answer – my gun didn't jam with her. Worked just fine. Suppose it'll jam with you?

(The **GUNMAN** *takes aim.)*

DICK. Wait! Can I ask you something?

GUNMAN. Sure.

DICK. What…what…

GUNMAN. Say it.

DICK. *(desperate – slowly finding his way)* What does it all mean? …I lost my girlfriend. My job. And my foot will never be the same. And now I can't help but think that maybe those who can engage in mindless small talk are the lucky ones. And that perhaps Bertolt Brecht was wrong. Maybe the best we can do is escape reality and avoid a life of the mind…

*(***DICK** *begins to sing.)*

(singing) IF WE CAN ESCAPE WHAT IS REAL
PERHAPS THEN WE WILL FIND
THAT THE GRIMNESS OF OUR CIRCUMSTANCE
CAN BE LEFT FAR BEHIND

(The **GUNMAN** *is unmoved.)*

DICK. *(speaking)* So tell me, what does it mean?

GUNMAN. *(beat)* That's…

DICK. Yes?

GUNMAN. That's a loaded question.

DICK. Huh?

GUNMAN. "What does it mean?" It's obvious that you assume that life has meaning. An unloaded question would be, "Do you think life has meaning?" See… that's…unloaded.

(The **GUNMAN** *aims point blank.* **DICK** *braces for the blast. Then…Eunice's cell rings with* What a Friend We Have In Jesus. **DICK** *jumps.)*

GUNMAN. What's that?

DICK. She forgot her cell phone.

*(***DICK*** picks up Eunice's cell phone.)*

DICK. It's a text message.

GUNMAN. Who from?

DICK. *(reading the message.)* It's…it's God.

GUNMAN. Really?

*(***DICK*** puts the open cell phone in the* **GUNMAN**'s *palm)*

GUNMAN. Hello?

(The sign sparkles to life. The **GUNMAN** *is so enthralled with the cell phone messages that he unconsciously hands the gun over to* **DICK**.*)*

(During the following **DICK** *crawls away.)*

(The text message floats in a sea of blue sky and white clouds. It reads:)

(– "What's Up?" –)

GUNMAN. God, is that you?

(– "☺" –)

It's been rainy.

(– "And It's Going To Rain Tomorrow, Too" –)

Will it stop?

(– "☺" –)

Good.

(– "Then It Will Rain Again ☹ " –)

Then what will happen?

(– "There Will Be Sun ☺ " –)

And then what?

(– *"Then It Will Rain ☹ "* –)

GUNMAN. *(cont.)* And then what?

(– *"More Sun ☺ "* –)

And then?

(– *"More Rain ☹ "* –)

That depresses me.

(– *"So?"* –)

…And then what will happen?

(– *"Then You Die"* –)

(With a flash and sparks the sign short-circuits. One of the chains holding the sign breaks and it half falls. Dangling from a single chain it dies.)

*(The **GUNMAN** falls on his knees weeping.)*

*(**DICK** manages to pull himself to his feet. He puts his hands in the air.)*

DICK. Don't shoot! I'm coming out!

*(**DICK** is hit with hundreds of flash bulbs as he leaves the building. **WALTER** the newscaster runs up.)*

WALTER. Dick Fig! You made it out alive!

*(**WALTER** shoves the microphone in his face.)*

DICK. *(confused and stunned)* Did I?

WALTER. Now that you've survived, can you tell us, what's God's purpose for you – in eight seconds or less.

DICK. Mary…

WALTER. She had to go to practice. The nation awaits your answer. What is God's purpose for you?

DICK. I…

WALTER. Yes, Dick?

DICK. I think…

WALTER. We only have a few moments until *Wheel of Fortune.* What is God's purpose for you?

(**DICK** *finally puts himself together, an answer comes to him, but just as he opens his mouth.*)

STAGE MANAGER'S VOICE. Hold please!

(*Blackout. Raucous Rock and Roll.*)

(*During the Curtain Call, Mary's baby carriage rolls all by itself across the stage.*)

THE END